4

THE HORSE from NOWHERE

BY ELIZABETH COATSWORTH

ARTWORK BY ED YOUNG

Holt, Rinehart and Winston, Inc.
New York Toronto London Sydney

A SATELLITE BOOK

Satellite Books are supplementary units designed for individualized, independent reading to accompany THE HOLT BASIC READING SYSTEM, by Bernard J. Weiss and Lyman C. Hunt.

GENERAL EDITORS
SATELLITE BOOKS

Lyman C. Hunt
Patricia Hynes Estill

For permission to reprint this story we wish to thank the original publisher, W. W. Norton & Company, Inc., and The World's Work (1913) Ltd. From Cricket and the Emperor's Son by Elizabeth Coatsworth, copyright © 1962 by Elizabeth Coatsworth. Used by permission.

Long ago there lived a boy in a house far up on a mountain. It was a lonely place of mists and pine trees, of waterfalls and deer. From the house he could look north almost to the borders of China.

"Beyond lies the desert," his father told him, "where the fierce men of the desert live in their tents. Sometimes they come into China like a swarm of hornets. They ride their shaggy ponies day and night without food or rest. And they kill everyone they meet with."

"Spare us from the swords of the Mongols!" sighed the boy's mother.

"It is many years since they have come," said his father. "Perhaps they have gone far away, herding their mares. Perhaps they will never return. They are like clouds, or the wind."

"What lies over there?" asked the boy, looking towards the south.

His father was silent, but his mother said, "There lies Peking, that great city."

"How far is it away?" asked the boy.

"A long day's ride." It was now his father who answered. "It is better not to think of it. It is nothing to us.

"And we are nothing to Peking," he added to himself, so low that the boy scarcely heard him.

So they lived, looking over peak and valley, fields and villages, far-off temples and yellow rivers. The boy never asked again about what lay to the north and south of them. But he often thought of the desert and the Mongols on their shaggy horses, and of Peking, that great city.

Although there were stables which belonged to the house where the boy lived, there were no horses in them. He did not ask where the horses had gone. There were many questions that he did not ask. Usually he and his father and mother dressed in coarse blue cotton, like the old man and woman who lived with them. They helped carry water from the spring. They worked with the old couple in the garden, to grow food, and his mother's flowers. They were up at dawn, and early to bed.

But on New Year's Day the father and mother were dressed in fine silks, and the dinner was served on beautiful plates. The boy saw everything but he said nothing.

And there were in the house a few beautiful pieces of jade wrapped and put away in a carved box. On rainy days his mother sometimes showed them to him. Now and then, he missed a piece. But he did not ask where it had gone.

There were besides the jade a few other beautiful things in the house. What the boy loved most of all was a painting on a scroll. It showed a black horse, harnessed and bridled, as if ready for his rider. The horse lifted his head impatiently. The wind seemed to stir his long mane. And with one hoof he pawed the ground.

Every morning when he was alone, the boy went to greet the little black horse. It seemed to him that the horse knew him. Did an eye move? Did an ear twitch? The boy could not have said. And yet it seemed to him that every morning the horse greeted him from the scroll on which he was painted.

But one morning the scroll was gone. The boy could not believe it. He looked on all the walls. No, the scroll had not been hung in a different place. He ran, stumbling, to the carved chest. No, the scroll had not been put away with the jade.

He ran to the door. There by the gate his father stood talking with the old man. The old man had his long staff in his hand. He was about to walk down the steep road to the village for supplies. Hours later he would climb back with a load of salt and tea and rice for the household.

It was always after the old man had gone to the village that the boy missed one of the pieces of jade.

Now he ran out to the gate. Carefully wrapped, he saw the scroll in the old man's hand.

"Father," he begged. "Do not send away the little horse! I will eat nothing, almost nothing. I will work before dawn and after dark. I will do anything you wish. But oh do not, do not send away the little black horse!"

His father was surprised. The boy had never told anyone of how much he loved the painted scroll.

"Do not weep," his father said kindly. "The little horse shall not go. I will send something else in his place. Some day perhaps I shall have to get rid of him, too. But I promise you, he shall be the last of our treasures to go."

So the old man went down the mountain that morning carrying something else in his hand, and the little black horse returned to his place on the wall. But now the boy could not keep silence any longer. He found the old woman working by herself in the garden.

"Tell me," said the boy. "Who are we? Who are you and your husband? Why do we live here? Why do my father and mother sometimes wear cotton and sometimes wear silk? Why does my father turn sad when he speaks of Peking, that great city?"

The old woman put down the short hoe with which she had been working.

"Come, then," she said. "The time has come to speak, since for you the time has come to ask questions. Let us sit down by the spring where we can talk quietly." When they were seated, she said, "To begin with what is easiest to answer. I was your father's nurse, and the old man is my husband. When all the others left him, he and I remained."

"Why did the others leave him?" asked the boy.

"Your father was a great lord and lived at the Emperor's court at Peking," said the old woman. "More and more the Emperor asked his advice. At last it was only your father's advice that the Emperor wished to hear. Then the other lords became jealous. They, who had been his friends, turned against him. They whispered lies to the Emperor. At first the Emperor paid no heed to them but they went on. A word here, a shrug there, a raised eyebrow somewhere else! They repeated to the Emperor things that your father had said, but not as he had said them.

"So at last the Emperor's heart turned against your father. The other lords wished to have him put to death. But the Emperor would not give the order. So he sent him to this far-away house in exile."

"What is exile?" asked the boy.

"It is to be sent away to a place where one must stay. If your father went down to the village even, his life would not be safe. Only in this house to which the Emperor sent him is your father safe."

So then at last the boy understood everything. And he thanked the old woman. He thanked her for telling him. And he thanked her for her faithfulness to his father.

After that talk the boy often looked towards Peking, that great city, hidden by a fold of the mountains. And he thought about his father and the Emperor, and the court, and the crowded streets, and the noise and the gaiety. There lay the dust of the world. And there his father and mother and he belonged.

But meanwhile they lived quietly. There was beauty and space around them, but exiles are always a little sad.

One autumn day the boy came into the room where his father and mother sat in the dusk, after a day of work in the garden. She was singing a song which she had made up from her own heart, and as she sang she lightly struck the strings of an instrument which lay across her lap:

"The leaves fall,
The cold winds blow,
At night the deer call
In the forests below.

"The stream that so mightily
Bounded with spring,
Has hushed its great song
To a murmuring."

Then his father took the instrument, and from his heart he answered.

"The hawk that sits
In the desolate fells
Is still a hawk
Though he wears no bells,

"And the sword is a sword
With a sword's bright will
Though it lie in its scabbard
Dark and still."

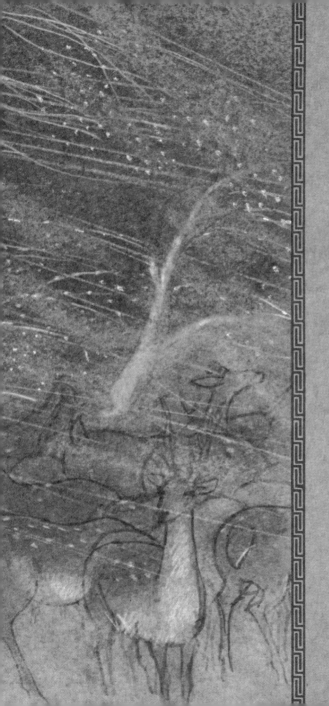

The boy would not have understood what the songs meant before his talk with the old woman. But now he knew that his mother compared his father to an autumn river, quiet and forgotten, and he knew that his father's song meant that his father had not changed, but was the same person he had been at the Emperor's court in the old days.

A great desire to sing a song, too, filled the boy and he, with a bow to his father, took the instrument and sang:

> *"When the nights are cold*
> *Close stand the deer,*
> *And the mice line their nests*
> *As winter draws near.*

> *"When the snow has covered*
> *Flower and fern*
> *In the braziers redly*
> *The fires burn!"*

The boy's parents were touched by this last song. A family's love for one another is warmest in bad times, the boy had reminded them. He had said it, too, with beauty.

"Ah, some day you will shine at court!" his mother cried, and then she put her hand to her mouth, and tears filled her eyes. The boy would never be seen at court. Like his father, he would live and die in exile.

Then one evening something happened. Coming in late from cutting wood, the boy saw a far-off band of fire to the north.

"Look, Father," he cried at the door. "What is this?"

His father came out and watched the fire for a little while, shading his eyes with his hand.

"The Mongols have come again," he said. "They are killing and burning as they go. Who will take news to the Emperor? Only we, on our mountaintop, have had the warning."

Running into the house he pulled on his long leather boots and snatched up a short fur jacket and cap, for the night was cold.

"But if you go into the valley, they will kill you," wept his wife.

"Even so, I must carry the warning," said her husband.

He was gone, and the boy and his mother listened to his footsteps stumbling down the dark mountainside.

"It is his duty," wept the boy's mother, "but oh, I fear that it is his death."

But what was that? There was a whinny from the courtyard and hoofs stamped the cobbles. In the light of the door stood a beautiful black horse with saddle and bridle of scarlet silk. As the boy came near, the horse bent his head.

The boy had never ridden a horse, but he seemed to know just what to do. No sooner was he in the saddle, than the horse had leaped forward into the darkness. But he made nothing of darkness nor of the roughness of the way. Smooth as a swallow in flight, he galloped on, down down down the mountainside. Once he neighed, and a shadow leaped from their path. The boy knew that it was his father, but in vain he tried to pull in his mount. On down the mountain they swept. Through the sleeping village they thundered and on on on, along the highway now, towards Peking, that great city.

The ride was like a dream. Never did the horse falter in his speed until they halted before the

gates of the palace. Torches flared. Officers of the guard ran forward. A messenger hurried to waken the Emperor. And soon the boy was led through seven courtyards, followed by the horse.

There in the last of the seven courtyards, the Emperor stood on a balcony lighted by lanterns. He listened to the boy's tale. Soon troops were pouring out of the city towards the north.

"Now these Mongols will be taught their lesson," said the Emperor. "They will be caught before they can finish their work and escape back into their deserts. But tell me," he added kindly, "who are you, who have saved so many villages?"

Then the boy bowed humbly and told the Emperor his name and his father's name.

"I have been mistaken," said the Emperor. "Only from a loyal father could such a son have sprung. In reward for this night, your father shall be restored again to all his honours. He shall return to my side. Never again shall I listen to lies whispered against him."

So the boy was led away to bed. And his horse was led away to the finest stall in the Emperor's stables. Perhaps the horse slept well. But it was a long time before the boy fell asleep. Over and over in his tired brain he asked himself, "Where

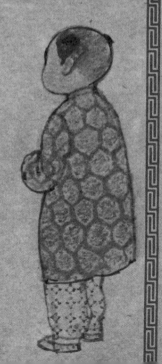

have I seen this horse before? And why did he appear out of nowhere to help us?"

But he was tired and at last he fell asleep.

At dawn he woke, and hurried off to see the black horse. But in the stables he was met by confusion and outcry. The grooms had but closed their eyes for a moment's sleep, the cocks had crowed, and when they awoke, blinking in the first light, lo! the black horse was gone!

All day the search went on, but not a single trace of the horse was found. The next day the Emperor ordered one of his finest steeds given to the boy, and he rode home, his heart torn between joy and sorrow. It would be a joy to tell his father that his exile was over. But how could he ever forget his grief at the loss of the black horse?

At last in the late dusk he was home again. The old man led away the Emperor's fine horse to the empty stable. His father and mother rose from their chairs to greet him. All was the same. Even the beloved scroll of the little horse hung in its usual place on the wall.

But suddenly he knew why the black horse which had carried him to Peking had seemed familiar. There he stood, scarlet saddle, bridle, blowing mane and all!

As the boy told his father and mother all the tale, the old woman listened. At the end she nodded.

"So that was it," she said. "When the young master rode away I happened to lift my candle to the scroll. It was empty. But I was so frightened for the master and the young master, that I said nothing. Still I went back at dawn to make sure. Everything was just as usual. So I thought I must have been dreaming after all."

From that day on, all went well with the boy and his father and mother and the old man and the old woman. They lived in a vast house in Peking, that great city. The father was once more high in the Emperor's favour, and the house was filled with treasures, but the greatest and most honoured of all the treasures was the scroll of silk upon which was painted a little black horse, saddled and bridled and pawing the ground, as though impatient to be off.